SCOOBY-DOO! and YOU:

A Collect the Clues Mystery

THE CASE OF THE THEATER PHANTOM

By Vicki Erwin

WORLDWIDE PUBLISHING™

SCHOLASTIC INC.
New York   Toronto   London   Auckland   Sydney
Mexico City   New Delhi   Hong Kong

To my daughter, Libby

ISBN 0-439-21753-9

12 11 10 9 8 7 6 5 4 3 2   0 1 2 3 4 5/0

Cover and interior illustrations by Duendes del Sur
Cover and interior design by Madalina Stefan

Printed in the U.S.A.

First Scholastic printing, October 2000

"**G**ood to see you again! Over here! Come join us," Daphne calls out as you enter the restaurant.

You have to walk around the mariachi band strolling the dining room, serenading customers as you cross to the table occupied by Scooby and the Gang. Fred pulls out a chair for you and you sit down.

"Like, where's the hot sauce?" Shaggy calls out as he and Scooby empty one basket of tortilla chips after another.

The waiter sets down a red bowl in front

of them. "Here's the specialty of the house, boys, our three alarm deluxe hot sauce."

"Rumm! Rot rauce," Scooby says as he dips a chip into the bowl and then sticks it into his mouth. Scooby's eyes grow big and steam comes out of his ears as he crunches, then swallows. He waves a paw in front of his mouth, then drinks his glass of water and Shaggy's. "Rot!" he pants.

"Wimp!" Shaggy dips two chips in the dish and pops them into his mouth. "Ye-oww!" he yells.

"I think I'll stick with the mild sauce," Velma says.

"Me, too," Daphne echoes. "I've had enough excitement this week."

"We've just solved another mystery at the Palace Theater down the street," Velma explains.

Scooby nods, his mouth too full of tortilla chips to talk.

"You probably would have enjoyed working on it with us," says Fred. "You look like you enjoy a good mystery now and then."

"Want to give it a try?" Daphne asks pulling out a colorful notebook and handing it to you.

"Absolutely!" you say, your voice squeaking a bit with the excitement of solving a real mystery.

"This is our Clue Keeper. We take turns writing down what happens in our mysteries and this time it was my turn," Daphne tells you. "Read it and try to figure out the mystery as you go along."

Fred leans closer. "Here are some hints. Every time we met a suspect, Daphne marked it with 👁👁 . When we found a clue, she marked it with 🔦 ."

"When you get to the end of my entries," Daphne adds, "we'll help you try to make some sense of what happened."

"Do you have your own Clue Keeper with you?" Velma asks.

You nod and pull it slowly out of your backpack. As much as you want to solve the mystery, you're a little nervous in front of the gang. After all, they're experts.

"Hey, if we can do it, you can do it too." Daphne pats you on the shoulder and gives you an encouraging smile.

Clue Keeper Entry 1

"Like, Daphne, are you sure we have to wear these silly bow ties?" Shaggy asked me, pulling a wild-patterned silk bow tie he'd slipped over his T-shirt away from his neck.

"Reah, ro re?" Scooby pulled at his bow tie, too.

"This is a formal gala," I reminded them as Fred helped me and Velma out of the Mystery Machine.

"Everyone looks great," Velma assured all of us as she swirled her floor-length red pleated skirt.

"They'll think we're the stars of the

show," I added as I adjusted the silk shawl over my long purple dress and led the way down the red carpet that stretched from the curb to the door of the Palace Theater.

"We must be early," Fred remarked. "There aren't many people around."

A single flashbulb popped as we entered the lobby of the newly restored theater. It was magnificent! The dark burgundy walls were covered with vintage posters of former shows in gold frames. A staircase with beautifully carved railings curved along one side of the lobby.

"Daphne! I'm so glad you could join us." Mr. Antoine Anthony, a friend of my parents, called to me from across the room. He mopped his forehead with a large, silk handkerchief as he motioned for us to join him.

"Thank you. I'd like you to meet my friends," I said, presenting the gang. "Gang, this is Mr. Antoine Anthony, the genius behind the restoration of the Palace Theater."

"I'm not feeling much like a genius at this point," Mr. Anthony confessed. "I sent hundreds of invitations to all the key people in the arts community, not to mention the press, and the turnout is . . . a bit disappointing." He dabbed at his brow again. "But, as they say, the show must go on!" Mr. Anthony smiled weakly.

"Why do you think the turnout is so low?" Fred asked.

"Fear, plain and simple fear," Mr. Anthony answered. "People are afraid that there will be a repeat of the last performance given at the Palace. You kids are probably too young to remember and it was before I came

to town, but the final show here at the theater had a surprise ending no one expected."

"You can't stop there," I said, wanting to know what had happened. "Tell us about it."

Mr. Anthony looked around nervously. "When it closed, the Palace Theater had a core cast of players starring in the shows here — Dolores Daytona was the leading lady and Thomas Smithson was the leading man. Right before the last show, Tommy showed up in Dolores's dressing room with a huge diamond ring and asked her to marry him. He said that he knew she couldn't act like she was so much in love with him day after day unless she truly was.

"Dolores told him she was sorry, but she didn't feel the same way. She explained her plan to go to Hollywood and become a movie star.

"Tommy disappeared that very evening. His understudy had to go on in his place."

"That doesn't sound too scary," Fred said.

"That isn't the end of the story. At the end of the first act, eerie music drowned out the players' final lines, followed by sobs.

'Doloooorresss!' the voice moaned, 'my looove!'" I wrapped my shawl a little tighter. Scooby moved between me and Fred and I felt him trembling.

"Was it Smithson?" Fred asked.

Mr. Anthony shook his head. "No one could find him — in fact no one has seen him since that night — but the director assured the audience it was a prank. Then in the middle of the final act, the lights went out, the same scary music started again, and a red rose drifted down from the balcony to land on the stage at Dolores Daytona's feet. As she leaned over to pick it up, someone or something swooped down from the balcony to the stage!"

Shaggy pushed in between Fred and me, too.

"Are you speaking of my final performance in this magnificent theater?" A tall, willowy woman wearing a silver dress that matched her silver hair fluttered up to us, cooing at Mr. Anthony.

"Telling them the story of the phantom, my dear," Mr. Anthony said, putting his arm around the older woman's shoulder. "And this is the legendary Dolores Daytona herself," he said.

Miss Daytona continued to talk only to Mr. Anthony, acting as if we weren't even standing there. "That dreadful story! Will it never die? That face — white, completely white with two eyes shining — has haunted my nightmares for years and years. Before every performance I'd received one perfect red rose with a card that read *From your biggest fan.* I found it flattering. But once I found out what had been sending them, I hated the sight of red roses. And if there is any sign this evening of that awful creature, I will be gone before you can say Academy Award." She paused and I jumped right in.

"Miss Daytona, I'm so pleased to meet you," I gushed, holding out my hand toward her. "My parents have told me so much about you!"

Miss Daytona ignored my hand. "Really, dear? Well, after you — and the movie producers we've invited — see my live performance, my name will be in every movie theater in the land!"

"I certainly hope that happens, my dear." Mr. Anthony patted Miss Daytona's hand then turned to us. "Let me finish the story. The phantom, as he was dubbed by the press, wore black and a flowing cape lined in red. 'My beautiful Dolores,' he said, 'you must remain in this theater or you will break my poor heart as you have broken the heart of Thomas. I cannot let you go.'"

"Was it Thomas Smithson?" Fred broke in.

"I am sure it wasn't him," said Miss Daytona. "The phantom claimed that the theater had been his home for many years and watching me had been his only joy. He grabbed me. . . ." Miss Daytona shivered.

"But I struggled and managed to break

away from him. The phantom turned to the audience," Miss Daytona continued.

"And he said . . . 'You will rue the day you left here!' With that he ran off the edge of the stage and swung back into the balcony. No one was able to catch him.

"Even after the theater was boarded up, neighbors heard strange noises. Occasionally, someone would find a wilted red rose in front of the stage door. Some of the construction workers also reported hearing and seeing odd things. But the show must go on. Right, Dolores?" Mr. Anthony said, pulling out his handkerchief and wiping the beads of sweat off his brow.

Dolores Daytona nodded slowly.

"The other strange thing is that the police found a small apartment off the balcony that looked like it had been occupied for quite some time. Yet no one admitted knowing about the apartment."

The story gave me goosebumps and I looked nervously around the brightly lit lobby. Everything appeared normal. "You think the phantom might show up tonight?" I asked. Scooby started shaking harder and hid behind my skirt.

"We've taken precautions to make sure everyone is safe," Mr. Anthony said quickly.

"We're not worried, are we?" Fred looked at us. Velma and I shook our heads.

Scoob peeked out from behind my skirt. I wasn't sure if he was shaking his head no or just shaking.

"Besides, you're in luck if there is any trouble," Velma said. "We're pros at dealing with this kind of thing."

"Right, pros," said Shaggy. "At getting out of the way!"

"I'm convinced everyone is safe or I wouldn't have reopened the theater," said Mr. Anthony. "Go ahead, kids, look around. We're still working on the balcony, so that's off limits, but you can even visit the stage before the show begins."

"And, like, where's the food?" Shaggy asked.

"Rood?" Scooby said, perking up and coming out from behind me.

"Refreshments are at the other end of the lobby," Mr. Anthony said with a laugh.

"Didn't you have some interviews set up for me?" I heard Dolores Daytona demand of Mr. Anthony as we walked away.

"There's a photographer outside. Didn't he take your picture?" Mr. Anthony said in a voice that trembled slightly.

"One photographer from a small local weekly won't give us the publicity we need, Antoine. We're going to have to make something happen here or all our hard work will be for nothing. And the programs? Where are they?" Dolores Daytona grabbed Antoine Anthony's arm and dragged him through a set of doors marked OFFICE.

Fred and Daphne's Mystery-Solving Tips

"**D**id you see the 👀 on page 9? Good. That means that you have at least one suspect. Write the answers to these questions in your Clue Keeper."

1. What is the potential suspect's name?

2. What does she do for a living?

3. What reason would she have for wanting the phantom to show up?

15

Clue Keeper Entry 2

"Let's take a look at that stage while we have a chance," Velma said.

"Good idea," Fred agreed.

"Hey, what about food?" Shaggy said.

"You can grab something and bring it along. We have to walk right by the refreshments," Velma said, pointing at the loaded tables.

"I'm glad that people decided not to come," Shaggy said as he and Scooby piled food high on their plates. "Means more for us, right Scoob?"

Scooby nodded.

As we walked down the aisle toward the stage, the sounds of Shaggy and Scooby chewing echoed off the walls in the nearly empty auditorium. The lights were dimmed and it took a few minutes for my eyes to adjust as the lobby doors swung shut behind us.

"Looks like we need to go through this door to get to the stage," I said, spotting an arched doorway to one side of the orchestra pit. We walked through the narrow entry single file with Scooby and Shaggy bringing up the rear.

"Where do you think you're going?" a man's voice snarled at us, scaring me into stopping without warning. Velma ran into me, Fred ran into her, and Shaggy and Scooby did a quick balancing dance to avoid dumping their plates all over Fred.

"Mr. Anthony said we could have a look at the stage before the show started," I explained. The man blocking our way was tall and thin with bushy black hair, thick eyebrows and a mustache. He wore a gray uniform and I realized that he was a security guard. His name tag said Smith in black letters.

"I'm not supposed to let anyone into the balcony area," the man growled at us. "There's wet paint."

"We weren't going to the balcony," Velma said.

Mr. Smith looked at us for a moment, then stepped out of our way. Fred, Velma, and I walked past him.

"Wait a minute. No food allowed backstage or onstage." Smith moved in front of Shaggy and Scooby.

Shag and Scoob cleared their plates in one big gulp and handed them to the guard.

"You haven't seen, like, any phantom-like creatures floating around?" Shaggy asked.

"Phantom, schmantom. Don't listen to Anthony's crazy stories," Smith said. "I've lived in this building for almost twenty years and haven't seen hide nor hair of a phantom."

"You like, live here?" Shaggy said, swallowing hard. "With the phantom?"

"I have myself a little apartment up in the balcony, nice and quiet and alone."

Smith frowned. "Can't say I'm all that happy that I'll be having guests every night from now on."

"I can't imagine that you would like that," Velma said.

Smith looked nervously toward the doorway. "Go ahead, have your look around. If no more folks than I see out there show up, I might not have to worry much about finding a new place to live."

"You'll be forced to move?" Velma asked.

We turned around as Dolores Daytona's voice drifted through the doorway. "And I assume my snack has been delivered to my dressing room?"

Miss Daytona and Mr. Anthony walked past and headed backstage, not even glancing our way. We turned back to the security guard.

"Mr. Smith," Velma started, but Mr. Smith was nowhere to be seen.

Velma's Mystery-Solving Tips

"**D**id you see another pair of 👁 👁 in this entry? That means you've found another suspect. Think about these questions and write the answers in your Clue Keeper:"

1. What is the potential suspect's name?

2. What does he do for a living?

3. Does he have a reason to keep people away from the theater?

Clue Keeper Entry 3

"Where did he go so fast?" I asked the gang.

"Maybe he's hungry," Shaggy answered.

"Or perhaps it's his job to deliver Miss Daytona's snack," Velma said quietly. "I don't think it would be a good idea to disappoint her."

"We probably don't have much time before the show starts," Fred said. "Let's look around while we can."

The five of us walked onto the stage. The curtain was closed so we couldn't see how many people had arrived.

"Hey, Scoob, there's an empty stage just waiting for us!" Shag said. He and Scooby did a soft shoe across the stage, jumping up and clicking their heels as the finale. Someone in the wings clapped.

"Can you do this?" a young girl asked. She jumped high into the air and turned a flip before she landed.

"Sandy Jordan!" I exclaimed. Sandy Jordan had been a world champion gymnast. I'd watched her compete — and win — on television dozens of time.

Sandy cartwheeled across the stage, landing directly in front of me and coming up with her hand outstretched. "Hi," she said, taking my hand and shaking it vigorously.

"What are you doing here?" Velma asked.

"I'm in the play," Sandy replied. "I play Dolores's daughter, although in truth, she's old enough to be my grandmother."

"I didn't know you were an actress, too," Fred said.

"It's my new career. And they wrote the part just for me, so there's gymnastics in it. The only trouble is Mr. Anthony is scared to death I'll fall, hurt myself, and sue him for millions of dollars and so they make me wear a silly harness — for my own protection." Sandy pointed at a contraption hanging across a beam in the ceiling.

"If they'd only let me have a bigger part ... but as long as Dolores has anything to say about it, I'll be hooked up and held back. I wish the phantom had taken her when he had the chance." Sandy grinned.

Shaggy glanced behind him and the rest of us laughed.

"Mr. Anthony swore that the phantom is a thing of the past," I said.

"Maybe yes, maybe no. I've seen a couple of things that have made me think it's not just a story," Sandy whispered, looking around. She motioned us to come closer.

"Someone left a single perfect red rose in my dressing room just like the phantom used to leave for Dolores Daytona."

Scooby jumped into Shaggy's arm and even I felt a little chill at Sandy's words.

Sandy laughed as she took in our reaction to her announcement. "It's almost showtime. See you later!" Sandy took a running jump, grabbed her safety harness and flew across the stage landing lightly on the other side.

Shaggy and Scooby's Mystery-Solving Tips

"Like, now there are three sets of  hanging out in this mystery. Did you see the new set on page 22? Cool. Why don't you answer these questions while Scooby and I . . . go hide from the phantom!"

1. What is the suspect's name?

2. What does she do for a living?

3. What is her reason for wanting the phantom to show up?

25

Clue Keeper Entry 4

"Maybe we'd better find our seats," I suggested.

"Good idea," Velma said.

Silently, we made our way down from the stage.

"Did any of you pick up a program?" I asked.

"I didn't see ushers or programs anyplace," Velma replied, looking around the audience. "Doesn't look like anyone has one."

"I'll sit in the middle," said Shaggy, waiting for me and Fred to take the end seats.

"That way if the phantom decides to walk down the aisle tonight, he'll have to crawl over you to get to me."

Scooby stepped in front of Velma and sat in the middle of the row beside Shaggy.

"I don't think you have anything to worry about," Velma said. "There's a security guard here to protect us. I don't know about you but I wouldn't try anything around Mr. Smith."

"But when Mr. Anthony was telling us about the phantom . . . it, like, gave me the creeps!"

"If you want to know what I think . . . " Fred paused.

"Go on," I urged.

"I think that they're bringing up that story all over again to start people talking about and thinking about the Palace Theater. You heard Dolores Daytona — 'We're going to have to make something happen here or all our hard work will be for nothing.' I'm curious to see if something does happen," Fred said.

"You've got a good point," said Velma. "Do

any of you wonder what happened to Thomas Smithson when Dolores Daytona gave him the kiss-off?"

"M-M-M-Maybe the phantom got him," said Shaggy, scooting lower in his seat.

"Reah, Rantom." Scooby slid down too.

"Don't forget that rose that Sandy Jordan said she received — like the one the phantom threw on the stage and gave to Dolores Daytona before each performance," I reminded them.

"Sandy may have made up that story to scare Miss Daytona away. I think there's some rivalry there," Velma said.

"But there were roses left at the stage door even after the theater closed," Fred said.

"Like, let's get out of here!" Shaggy stood up and started down the row.

"Sit down! The show's about to start!" a voice behind us whispered angrily.

"There are going to be refreshments at intermission," Velma said firmly to Shaggy and Scooby.

Shaggy sat back down in his seat and

Scooby straightened up.

The spotlight dimmed and classical music drifted out of the speakers mounted on each side of the stage. Antoine Anthony stepped out into the middle of the stage and the spotlight came up.

"Ladies and gentlemen, I'd like to welcome you back to the Palace Theater." Anthony bowed and everyone applauded.

"Not only is the theater better than ever, but the show we are about to present is going to be something that you'll be talking about for days to come. It will also be your privilege to witness the stage debut of world-class gymnast, Sandy Jordan.

Applause and cheers broke out at the mention of Sandy's name and we joined in.

"And it's the return of one of the most beloved of all stage and screen stars to that place she credits as the birthplace of her career.

"Ladies and gentlemen, she would like to say a few words to you before the start of the show — our star, Miss Dolores Daytona!" Mr. Anthony stepped back with a sweep of his arm as music swelled in the background.

I sat up a straighter to get a better look at Miss Daytona's entrance.

"Yes, ladies and gentlemen, Miss Dolores Daytona," Mr. Anthony repeated louder. He reached into his jacket pocket, pulled out his handkerchief, and started mopping his forehead.

The music changed suddenly, filling the auditorium with eerie sounds followed by deep sobs. A single red rose landed on the stage as the sobs rose in volume. I looked toward the balcony and gasped. A white featureless face with two blank eyes stared down upon the departing crowd. Someone or something balanced on the balcony rail. It raised its arms, displaying the red satin lining in its cape, drew the cape across its face, and fell backward, melting into the shadows.

"Like, it's the phantom!" Shaggy shouted. He and Scooby jumped over Velma and were the first ones out of the auditorium. They were soon followed by the rest of the audience.

"It is the phantom!" Fred confirmed as we ran after Shaggy and Scooby.

Clue Keeper Entry 5

By the time we reached the lobby it was empty. Outside, everyone was climbing into cars and driving away. Shaggy and Scooby had stopped in mid-flight at the deserted refreshment table.

"Jinkies!" Velma cried, "I never expected to see something like that!"

"Like, as soon as we build up a little strength, we're ready to get out of here," Shaggy said.

Mr. Anthony ran through the theater doors, calling, "Come back! Please all of you come back!"

At the same time, Smith the security guard stepped out from the door underneath the steps at the side of the lobby. "Wha — what happened?"

"The phantom!" Mr. Anthony said. "It's back! Where were you? It's your job to make sure that nothing like this would happen to spoil this night."

"You sent me to look for the missing programs! I was in the storage room," Smith explained.

"Did you find them?" Mr. Anthony asked.

Smith shook his head. "I'll keep looking."

"And Miss Daytona? Has anyone seen her? She never misses a chance to make a grand entrance." Mr. Anthony mopped his brow.

"What is going on here?" The doors to the theater burst open and Miss Daytona came through, her face bright red and her silver hair mussed. She was followed by Sandy Jordan.

"Dolores we were so worried! Where were you?" Mr. Anthony asked.

"Someone," Miss Daytona looked pointedly

at Sandy Jordan, "locked me in my dressing room."

"I let her out," Sandy said.

"Smith, what do you have to say for yourself?" Mr. Anthony whirled around to face the security guard.

But once again, Mr. Smith had disappeared.

"We should take a look around," Fred suggested. "Looks like Mr. Smith could use some help."

"He won't have a job much longer if I have anything to say about it," Dolores Daytona said. "I haven't even met the man and he's supposed to be protecting me."

"The theater, dear, it's his job to take care of the theater," Mr. Anthony said. "Why don't we step into my office and let Daphne and Fred and their friends have a look around? I would feel better if we stayed together until someone figures out what is going on."

"I'm going back to my dressing room. I'd rather take my chances with the phantom than Dolores," Sandy Jordan said, heading back toward the theater.

"That may not be a very good idea," I called after Sandy, but she was gone.

"Okay, gang, it will take us less time if we split up to look for clues," Velma said. "Daphne, Fred, you look around down here while Scooby, Shaggy, and I take a look in the balcony?"

"Balcony?" Shaggy said, backing away from us. "Isn't that like where the phantom lives?"

"We're only looking for clues," said Velma. "C'mon fellas, I'm sure if there was a phantom, he's gone by now."

"Easy for you to say," Shaggy mumbled.

Scooby gobbled another slice of cake and followed Shaggy and Velma up the steps.

We waited until everyone had left the lobby, then I tiptoed over to the door under the steps. "I'm wondering what exactly is under here and why Mr. Smith was there instead of in the theater."

"Let's see," Fred said.

He opened the door and we walked along the bare concrete floor. The lights were so far apart we could barely see.

As I walked along behind him, I heard a sound behind me. I stopped and the sound stopped. When I looked around, nothing was there. I took a few more steps and heard it again, swish swish swish.

"You hear that?" I whispered. "Listen."

I walked toward Fred.

Grinning, he pointed at my feet.

When I looked down I saw what was making the noise. A piece of paper was stuck to my shoe. I pulled it off. It was white paper with a ragged edge like it had been torn out of something . ⊶

"It could be a page out of one of the missing programs," I said, recognizing a young Dolores Daytona standing at the foot of the stairs above us. "It looks like it was taken here, but a long time ago. There's someone in the picture with her, but I can't see who it is."

"What are those black smudges?" Fred gently touched the paper, then rubbed his fingers together. "This stuff is sticky. I think it may be black paint — and still wet so it hasn't been here long!"

"You'd better try to wash it off before it dries," I said.

"Maybe there's a work-room this way," Fred said, taking the pa-per from me and starting down the hallway.

Fred tried door af-ter door, but all were locked until the very last one.

"We're in luck," he said, sticking his head inside, "there's a sink in here."

"What's that smell?" I asked, wrinkling my noise against the strong odor wafting out.

Fred stepped inside, turned on the water, and rubbed his hands together. "It's not coming off," he said. "But here's something I can try." He unscrewed the top from a bottle resting on the edge of the sink. The odor that had only been unpleasant before nearly knocked me over. I coughed and my eyes burned. I backed out into the hallway.

"It's not that bad," Fred said, pouring some into the palm of his hand, then rubbing them together. "Paint remover. Works like a charm." He rinsed his hands and dried them on a towel hanging beside the sink.

Fred pulled the door shut behind him. "Look! There's a staircase. Let's see where it goes. Maybe we'll run into the rest of the gang. We can see what they've found and ask them what they think about this," Fred held up the paper I'd pulled off my shoe.

"**D**id you see the  on page 36? That means you've found the first clue to the mystery. Write it down in your Clue Keeper. Think about these questions:"

1. What was the clue in this entry?

2. Where did the paper come from?

3. What was covered up by the black paint?

Clue Keeper Entry 6

"The balcony is huge!" Velma said when she, Shaggy, and Scooby had made their way up the grand staircase. "Shaggy? Scooby? Are you coming? Look around you! It's only us."

"Like, I've heard you say that before," Shaggy said, "just before something jumped out and started chasing us."

"You stay there then and look for clues at that end of the balcony and I'll look down here," Velma said walking to the front of balcony and looking over the edge of the railing. "I think this is about where I saw the phantom when I looked up. And look! I may have something here." She examined the railing closely.

"Okay, like what?" Shaggy asked, joining her. Scooby came a little more slowly, looking over his shoulder every few steps.

"Look at the marks in this paint — do they look like footprints to you? The phantom was standing on the railing." Velma touched the railing quickly with the tip of her finger. "Wet paint," she said. "Whoever was standing here must have black paint on his or her shoes after being here."

"Rook!" Scooby pointed at the worn carpeting.

"Black footprints!" said Velma, "but they don't go very far." She followed the shoe prints only few steps up the aisle.

"He must have taken his shoes off," said Shaggy.

Velma continued up the aisle. "No," she said, "that's not what happened. Look, there are papers on the floor although it looks like someone picked most of them up. Here's a couple that got kicked under a seat." She

leaned down and picked up some sheets of
paper that looked like they'd been trampled
a few times.

"Hey, stop that!" Shaggy said, rubbing
the side of his head.

"Stop what?" asked Velma, looking up
from the papers she held.

"Throwing stuff. Scoob, I mean it."

"Rot re," Scooby said.

"There's something on the floor," Velma
said, pointing.

"R-r-red rose petals?" Shaggy stammered.

"Ruh-roh," Scooby said.

Velma later told us she heard a whistling

42

sound followed by a thump and then saw a large black figure looming in front of Shaggy and Scooby. Shaggy and Scooby yelled and ran out the door and down the stairs.

Fred had his hand on the door at the top of the stairs when we heard their yells. They almost knocked us down when Fred opened the door.

The phantom ran forward and I was sure it was heading our way, but then it leaped over the balcony rail and swooped down to the floor of the theater. With a bone-chilling laugh, it tucked its head inside its cape and disappeared into the shadows.

Fred and I ran to the edge of the balcony, but the phantom was gone.

Velma joined us, clutching some papers. "Did you guys find anything?" she asked.

Fred showed her the page with the black paint smeared all over it.

"The phantom must have gone down into that hallway, then," Velma said. She showed us the pages with pictures cut out and covered in black footprints. "And the paint came off the railing."

"We need to get the gang together and try to put the pieces of this puzzle together," Fred said.

I couldn't have agreed more! The balcony was too creepy with just the three of us — and the threat of the phantom returning.

"Did you see the second 🔦 on page 41? That's the clue I found — with a little help from Scooby and Shaggy. Answer these questions in your Clue Keeper:"

1. What clue did you find in this entry?

2. Who could have left the footprints?

3. Where have you seen program pages like the one I found in the balcony?

Clue Keeper Entry 7

Fred, Velma, and I caught up with Shaggy and Scooby in the lobby.

"Those footprints in the wet paint on the balcony rail," said Velma, "make me think. Isn't the balance beam Sandy Jordan's specialty? It would take skill to balance on that railing."

"But why would Sandy want to bring back the phantom?" Shaggy asked.

"To scare Dolores Daytona away and have the spotlight to herself," I said.

"Whoever was near that railing would have black paint on their shoes and their hands too," Velma added, holding up her stained index finger.

"So we need to get a look at everyone's shoes?" I asked.

At that moment Sandy Jordan came into the lobby. "Have you seen Antoine or Dolores? I'd like to go on home if this show isn't going to happen.

Velma and I looked down at Sandy's feet. She had on white tennis shoes with no sign of black paint anyplace. Her hands and nails were clean and, if she'd used paint remover any time lately, my nose would have known that too!

"It was a pleasure to meet you guys," Sandy said. "Now, does anyone know where I can find the boss? By that I mean Antoine."

"Last time I saw them they were going to Mr. Anthony's office," I said.

"That's where I'll look then." Sandy knocked softly, then slipped inside.

"Are you kids still here?" Mr. Smith came out from under the steps, holding a laundry bag. "I'd like to lock up and get some sleep."

"We'll be going in a few minutes," Fred

said. "We have a few things to do. . . . "

"Hurry up and finish so I can put this evening behind me," Mr. Smith said.

Velma and I were looking at Mr. Smith's shoes. They looked as clean as Sandy's and he had on a clean uniform with black stripes down the legs of his pants. The laundry bag covered his hands so I couldn't get a good look at them.

Mr. Smith dropped the laundry bag near the front doors. "I only have two uniforms and Anthony wants me to wear a clean one for each show. Laundry truck should pick this up early in the morning," he mumbled.

Velma was studying a poster hanging on the wall of the lobby. "Mr. Smith!" she called after the security guard.

"What now?" he turned and faced her.

"Who hung these posters and marked

them with the shows and the dates?" Velma asked him.

"Like most everything else around here that gets done, I did it," Mr. Smith grumbled. He pulled the door closed behind him.

Velma continued to study the poster. "Come here," she said to me.

As I walked by the bag of laundry my eyes began to water and my nose wrinkled. "Fred, try to wash the smell of that paint remover off your hands again," I said.

"You can't smell me from across the lobby," Fred said. He had already joined Velma.

He was right. I smelled the air. I looked around. Then my eyes fixed on the laundry bag sitting near me. I bent down and sniffed. Holding my nose I backed away from it.

"Take a good look at this poster. Does this look like the same picture as this one?" Velma asked, holding up the pages we'd found earlier next to the poster.

I compared the two. Dolores Daytona was the same in both pictures. The person standing beside her was the same person blacked out by the paint on the page Fred and I had found and totally cut out of the one Velma, Shaggy, and Scooby had found. In the poster, the face of the man standing next to her — I could tell it was a man by the clothes — was covered by a banner with the show and the date it had been presented at the palace. "That must be Thomas Smithson next to her," I said.

"Are you thinking what I'm thinking?" Velma asked.

Fred and I nodded.

"It's time to set a trap for the phantom," Velma declared.

Shaggy and Scooby's Mystery-Solving Tips

"**D**id you, like, find a new clue in this entry? You can bet that the Scooby gang did, and we also figured out why it was important. Here are some questions that will help you figure it out too:"

1. What clue did you find in this entry?

2. What did the smell of Mr. Smith's bag remind Daphne of?

3. Why would Mr. Smith have paint remover on his uniform?

Clue Keeper Entry 8

In a few minutes we had a plan, but it took awhile to talk Shaggy and Scooby into helping us.

"You guys looked so great up on that stage earlier, we'd like to see it all again," I said.

"You mean, like, dancing?" asked Shaggy.

"That's exactly what we mean," said Velma. "We want Mr. Anthony to have a look, maybe put you in one of his shows."

"We were that good?" Shaggy asked.

"You were fabulous!" I said.

"Like, why do I think there's more to it than that?" Shaggy asked.

"We need someone to go into the theater again and see if the phantom will come out," Fred explained.

"Zoinks! And then?" Shaggy asked.

"We'll catch him and find out who's scaring everyone away from the theater," Velma said.

Scooby hid behind my skirt again.

"Scooby? We need you, too," said Velma.

"Ruh-uh," Scooby said.

"Would you do it for a Scooby Snack?" Velma asked.

"Ruh-uh," said Scooby.

"How about three Scooby Snacks and as many tacos as you can eat when we catch the phantom?" Fred asked.

"Rokay," Scooby agreed. He came out from behind my skirt and held the door open for Shaggy and rest of us.

While we worked backstage, Shaggy and Scooby were center stage clowning around. We heard the doors to the theater open and footsteps come down the aisle.

Eerie music filled the auditorium. "Goooo awaaaay!" a voice came out of the speakers. Then, one red rose fell from the balcony and another and another. I heard a swish and the phantom landed on the stage with a thump. It was about to swoop down on Scooby when Fred lowered the curtain. The phantom fought against the folds of the velvet curtain becoming more and more entangled the more he fought.

"You caught him!" Dolores Daytona and Antoine Anthony ran down the aisle.

"Would you like to see who's been scaring people away from your theater?" I asked Mr. Anthony.

"With pleasure." And Mr. Anthony pulled off the curtain and unmasked the phantom.

"Bring Scooby another plate of tacos," Fred says to the waiter.

"What did you think of our latest case?" Daphne asks. "Now that you know the suspects and have a list of the clues, do you know who was pretending to be the phantom?"

"I think I know," you answer.

"I'll bet you're right," Velma says. "But here's a few things to think about. Look at your list of suspects and decide who might have a reason to scare people away from the theater."

"Then, ask yourself who could have been responsible for the clues we found," says Fred.

"And finally, who had the opportunity to be the phantom?" asks Velma.

"You may want to eliminate suspects first — any of the suspects who didn't have a reason, the ability to do what the phantom did, or the chance to do it," Daphne says.

The waiter arrives with Shaggy and Scooby's tacos. "What are those little green things on that platter?" asks Shaggy.

"Jalapeño peppers," answers the waiter. "They're hot," he adds.

"They look good. Give me some," Shaggy says.

Shaggy pops the pepper into his mouth, chews, and swallows. "Yeow! Fire! Fire!" he shouts, grabbing water glasses and drinking them thirstily.

Scooby laughs.

"You need a few more minutes?" Daphne asks.

You nod.

"Take all the time you need, then we'll compare answers," says Fred.

Jinkies! It's time for you to guess whodunnit. Do you think you know who it is? When you're ready, turn the page and discover the ending of *The Case of the Theater Phantom.*

"It was Mr. Smith, the security guard," says Velma.

"Who wasn't really Mr. Smith, but Thomas Smithson, Dolores's former leading man," Daphne explains.

"Dolores Daytona wanted publicity for her new show, but she had been locked in her dressing room when the phantom appeared the first time and she was in Mr.

Anthony's office the second time we saw it," Velma says.

"Sandy Jordan could have walked along the balcony rail and swooped down in the harness that she showed us. Yes, it was the same one the phantom used," Daphne says. "But why would she tear pages out of the programs?"

"Our first clue was the page torn out of the program. All of the programs had disappeared and yet here was a page out of one," says Fred.

"Then in the balcony, we found footprints in the wet paint and something cut out of more program pages. The phantom must have torn the pages out of the program and cut them up," Daphne continues.

"When I took a good look at the posters on the walls of the lobby and saw that there was a banner across everyone of them, it made me suspicious," Velma explains.

Daphne cut in. "Then there was Mr. Smith's laundry bag that smelled like paint remover, and the fact he had changed his clothes in the middle of the evening. Could he have gotten paint on his pants and tried to clean it off with the remover?"

"Did anyone else notice that every time Dolores Daytona showed up, Mr. Smith disappeared?" Velma asks.

"I thought Mr. Smith wanted everyone out because it was his home — he'd told us he'd lived there for over twenty years," Fred reminds you.

"But, it wasn't. The phantom was really the brokenhearted Thomas Smithson. He had created his own world in the theater years ago and he wanted Dolores to be a part of it. When she refused, Smithson as the phantom intended to kidnap Miss Daytona and hold her prisoner in the theater where she'd be his and his alone," Velma explains.

"But that didn't work either, so he got a job as the caretaker and continued to live alone in the theater, waiting for Dolores to come back," Daphne says.

"This isn't the last you'll hear about the Palace Theater," says Fred. "Mr. Anthony is selling the story to all the national magazines. I don't think he'll have to worry about people showing up for the next show."

Velma turns to you. "Did you figure out whodunnit?" she asks.

"Come back again," says Fred. "We like to discuss our cases with up and coming detectives."

"Maybe we'll even run into you at the Palace Theater," says Daphne. "Mr. Anthony has added a few new scenes to the play."

"Yeah, Shaggy and Scooby are going to do their soft shoe to open the show," Fred says.

"And, like, we're getting paid in desserts left over from the grand reopening. Yumm!" says Shaggy. "Right, Scoob?"

"Rooby Rooby Roo!" Scooby agrees.